THIS BOOK BELONGS TO

....

**For Georgie, who adores super cute
characters and furry animals.**

First published in Great Britain 2021 by Egmont Books

An imprint of HarperCollins*Publishers*

1 London Bridge Street, London SE1 9GF

egmontbooks.co.uk

HarperCollinsPublishers

1st Floor, Watermarque Building, Ringsend Road Dublin 4, Ireland

Text copyright © 2021 Egmont Books UK Ltd

Illustrations by Dynamo © 2021 Egmont Books UK Ltd

Special thanks to Rachel Delahaye
Text design by Janene Spencer
With thanks to Speckled Pen for their help in the development of the series.

ISBN 978 0 7555 0124 3

Printed and bound in Great Britain by CPI Group

1

MIX
Paper from
responsible sources
FSC™ C007454

This book is produced from independently certified FSC™ paper
to ensure responsible forest management.

For more information visit: www.harpercollins.co.uk/green

SUPER CUTE

BEST FRIENDS
FOREVER

PIP BIRD

EGMONT

THE WORLD OF SUPER CUTE

HUG WHALES

SNOOZY HOLLOW

SANDY BEACHES

SMILEY SUNFLOWER FIELD

DIPSY DAISY MEADOW

CHARM GLADE

FLOWER TREE STABLE

WISH TREE

LUCKY'S HOME

CORNUCOPIA AVENUE

PINK LEMONADE HOT TUB

MARZIPAN LANE

SHOPS

MANE STREET

CLIVE'S HOME

THE BLOSSOM FESTIVAL

VANILLA VALLEY

RITZY AVENUE

THE MARSHMALLOW CANYON

DEE'S HOME

MOMII

THE MUSEUM OF MOST IMPORTANT ITEMS

CONTENTS

CHAPTER ONE

We're Glowing to Charm Glade!

Lucky the lunacorn had an invitation in her bag to a *very* special occasion. It was taking place on the other side of Charm Glade and she had been flying all night to get there! But when sunrise came, Lucky just had to stop. The World of Cute was waking up and it was an amazing thing to watch.

Lucky landed in the Dipsy Daisy Meadow and gazed happily as the golden beams tickled the multi-coloured grasses. Flowers lifted their sleepy heads, little creatures emerged from their dens and birds rose from the treetops, swooping and singing. The start of a new day was always enchanting. But today, as distant music drifted on the breeze, Lucky sensed something especially magical in the air.

'I must be close to Charm Glade!' she said to herself.

'I must be close to Charm Glade!' repeated a chorus of voices.

Lucky felt a bit confused. Then she spotted long ears and cotton tails in the grass around her. 'Oh, it's the funny bunnies!' she said.

'Funny bunnies!' the bunnies giggled, springing one by one from the undergrowth like popcorn. They stopped in mid-air to do star jumps and cartwheels, before tumbling back down again. Lucky watched in awe.

A green bunny sprang forward. 'Charm Glade is just a few leaps that way. Or *flaps*,' it added, spotting Lucky's wings. It looked down at Lucky's hooves. 'Or gallops . . . What kind of creature *are* you?'

'A lunacorn,' Lucky replied.

'A lunacorn,' gasped the bunnies. 'Wow!'

'I'm like a unicorn, but with a very special horn,' Lucky explained.

The bunnies stared in confusion at the normal-looking horn on the top of Lucky's head.

'It's not doing anything now,' said Lucky. 'But when the moon comes out, it *glows*!'

'**WOW!**' said the bunnies again.

Lucky had always known that one day her horn would glow and be ready to perform magic. She had waited so long for it to happen, she worried it never would! But that very night, as the moon rose high, her horn had dazzled for the very first time. Lucky had been so excited, she'd swooped through the air, twisting and turning like an acrobatic star. Her glowing horn was now guiding her through the marshmallow canyons toward Charm Glade.

Now that her horn had started to glow, it meant the magic was brewing. And surely it wouldn't be long before Lucky discovered what that magic would be . . .

'It will happen when the time is right,' her mum had said.

Lucky hoped the right time would happen soon. And she REALLY hoped her horn would do something super cool!

'Are you going to the Blossom Festival?' asked an orange bunny.

Lucky nodded. 'And this year I'm entering the Cuteness Competition.'

'You *are* quite cute,' said a white bunny, ears turning pink as she blushed.

'Thank you very much,' said Lucky. 'So are you! But the Cuteness Competition is not about what you look like. It's a contest to show everyone what makes you special.'

'And what makes *you* special?' the white-and-pink bunny asked.

'My horn, of course!' Lucky laughed. 'I must be on my way now. Nice to meet you all. Bye!'

The bunnies tumbled like bouncy balls back into the grasses and Lucky took off into the sky, to continue her journey among the candyfloss clouds.

As the sun rose higher, the World of Cute burst into colour. Candy blossoms popped open in the heat. Lucky was flying above a Smiley Sunflower Field when she saw an irresistible sight – a crystal-clear pond.

'Surely another quick stop won't hurt,' she said to herself.

She landed and dipped her head to drink. The water was sweet and cold, instantly washing away her tiredness.

I'm refreshed and ready for the competition! Lucky thought. Now to check the details . . .

Lucky pulled the slip of paper from the

backpack and was opening her invitation when, all of a sudden, strange noises erupted behind her. Rustles, snuffles and whistles. They seemed to be coming from a single sunflower – a sunflower with its petals still closed. Lucky crept closer and saw a tiny snoring sushi-mouse cradled inside.

'Hello, little –' she began.

'**SHHH**. Don't wake Dylan! He's v-e-r-y grumpy in the mornings!'

The owner of the voice sprang from nowhere and landed at Lucky's feet. Actually it landed ON Lucky's feet. She squeaked in surprise and dropped her invitation. It was . . . a pineapple! And it was wearing goggles!

To Lucky's horror, the breeze snatched up her invitation and blew it towards the water.

'Pip to the rescue!' shouted the pineapple.

It back-flipped over the pond and then triple-flipped back. Then it did a forward roll and presented Lucky with the piece of paper, speared on its spiky green top. The invitation was only a tiny bit soggy.

'Thank you. How did you *do* that?' Lucky gasped.

'Pine-ninja,' said the pineapple. 'Ninja training for pineapples. I'm Pip. And you must be Lucky.'

'You're a mind-reading pineapple too?'

'No, I saw your name on the top of the invitation,' Pip said with a giggle. 'How exciting – you're entering the Cuteness Competition!'

Lucky kicked her back heels with joy. It *was* exciting. The competition wasn't big enough for the whole World of Cute to enter together, so invitations were sent out randomly. It was like a lucky dip. Eventually everyone would get a turn, but this was Lucky's first ever invite.

'What's your cuteness trick?' Pip asked, spinning on the spot and tripping over her feet.

'I'm hoping my horn will perform some cute magic,' Lucky said. 'You should enter the competition too!'

Pip backed into the flowers, knocking some glittery pollen on to her head. She sneezed loudly. 'I . . . I'm not . . . I don't even have an invitation.'

'There *might* be a free space,' said Lucky. 'Or just come along for fun!'

Pip lifted her goggles. Her little eyes were

scared. 'But I've never been as far as Charm Glade on my own before.'

'You won't be on your own if you come with me,' Lucky said. 'We'll fly there together.'

Pip blinked three times, nodded, and did a backwards somersault on to Lucky's back. She somehow managed to land on her head, rather than her bottom.

'Ooh, sorry!' she said with a laugh, turning the right way up. 'I'm still perfecting my pine-ninja skills, you see. Let's go!'

'That's the spirit!' Lucky laughed. 'Hold tight . . .'

'Can we go fast?' said Pip. 'I don't like being in the sun.'

'But Pip, pineapples are tropical fruits!'

'I know!' Pip grinned. 'But the heat makes me feel extra prickly.'

A little cloud suddenly descended from the sky and hovered right above them, creating a perfect puddle of shade.

Lucky cheered. 'This is our lucky day! A cloud has appeared just for you, Pip, so it's nice and cool. Charm Glade, here we come!'

The happy lunacorn spread her wings, but was stopped by a loud voice. It was slow and low, like a talking yawn.

'WAIT!'

'Who said that?' asked Lucky, looking all around her.

'Did-you-know-that-a-sunflower-head-can-have-as-many-as-two-thousand-seeds?' It was the same deep voice, but it was now talking really quickly.

Lucky frowned at a bird fluttering out of the sunflowers and flying away. No, the bird hadn't said anything. Then what had spoken?

A creature came rolling out of the flower field and on to the bank in front of Lucky and Pip. Its yellow fur quickly turned grass-green.

'What is it?' Pip asked. 'My goggles are too dark to see.'

'I don't know,' said Lucky. 'It changes colour. It's now rubbing its eyes with one hand, and with the other it's scratching its . . . never mind.'

'That's sounds like Sammy the Sloth,' Pip said. 'Always got an itch somewhere.'

Sammy pushed up his glasses and opened his mouth wide. Lucky was expecting a giant

yawn (sloths were VERY sleepy creatures!) and was surprised when a sudden rush of words came out instead.

'Did you know the Blossom Festival is inspired by the peach blossom at Wild Wood that dances on the wind? Did you know the Cuteness Competition is the longest-running competition in the World of Cute? One hundred years old, same age as my great-grandfather Sammy, who I'm named after. Boy, that sloth can talk. Now, where was I? Ah yes, the competition. It's the best thing about the Blossom Festival, apart from the candied nuts stall. I remember the finest act I ever saw was a trumpeting cheese. Won it twice. But nobody has ever won it more than twice. So Clive probably won't win again. No matter what he thinks!'

'Who's Clive?' Lucky asked, trying to keep up.

'Clive the chihuahua,' Pip explained. 'He wants to be the first to win three times in a row.'

'He got an invitation three years running?' Lucky said. 'That's incredibly lucky!'

'It's not luck,' said Pip. 'His ancestors first established the Cuteness Competition and now he claims the right to enter every year. We should talk quietly in case he hears us, because he's v-e-r-y competitive and he can be quite mean.'

'You can say that again,' Sammy said, rolling his huge eyes. 'He's been known to noodle-ify contestants he thinks have a chance of winning.'

'Noodle-ify?' Lucky quizzed.

'Tie up with noodles,' Pip explained. 'Ooh, and do you remember the time he cake-ified Plumpkin, Sammy?'

'Ah yes, poor Plumpkin the puffer fish!' said Sammy. 'Clive surrounded his house with magic temptation cakes and Plumpkin ate himself silly. Couldn't move for a week. Too puffed up. He missed the contest.'

'So if this Clive hears us talking, we might be noodle-ified or cake-ified?' Lucky gasped. 'Well, that's just mean. There's no place for mean at the Blossom Festival.

We won't let his sneaky tricks scare us!'

'Shall we get going, to be on the safe side?'
Pip said nervously.

'Good idea, Pip.' Lucky drew her hoof
across the ground, preparing for take-off.
'Sammy, why don't you come with us?' she
said, looking at the sloth. 'It's the most exciting
event in the World of Cute calendar. You don't
want to miss it!'

'Wonderful idea,' Sammy said brightly. 'I
have no intention of entering – competitions are
not for me! – but I'll come along if there's room
for another little one?'

He climbed on to Lucky's back, leaned
against Pip and promptly fell asleep.

'Are we ready?' Lucky called. 'Next stop, Charm Glade!'

Off to the competition with new friends, she thought happily. This is going to be the best day ever!

CHAPTER TWO

The Trouble with Tutus

'I'm f-f-flying!' Sammy gasped, suddenly waking up as Lucky took off. 'The record for the fastest flying creature without wings is the dilly toad, who once leaped at the speed of light after stepping on a drawing pin.'

Lucky laughed. 'You're full of wonderful facts, Sammy,' she said. 'I can't fly at the speed of light, but I wish I could. After all our chatting,

I'm worried we'll be late for the Cuteness Competition.'

'Come on, Sammy,' Pip said, giving the sloth a squeeze. 'Do you know a short-cut?'

Sammy yawned. 'Yes, I do, as a matter of fact. Lucky, go left here!'

Lucky leaned to the left, laughing as her companions made *whoa* noises and held tighter to her mane.

'Look, the cloud came with us!' Pip said, looking at the little cloud still above their heads. 'Hey, up there! Are you following us?'

The cloud stretched, puffed and wriggled. Out popped little eyes and a shy smile. 'You said you wanted shade,' she whispered.

'And I was feeling a little lonely.'

Pip whispered something in Sammy's ear. Sammy leaned forward and whispered something in Lucky's ear. Then Lucky whispered something to Sammy, who whispered it back to Pip.

The pineapple looked up at the cloud and grinned. 'We'd love you to join us on our journey,' she said. 'I'm Pip, this is Sammy and our pilot is Lucky the lunacorn. What's your name?'

'Cami.' The little cloud smiled a bigger smile than before. 'Do you mind if I stay close to your head? I don't like heights.'

'Not at all,' Pip said. 'But be careful of–'

'OW!' Cami cried as Pip's prickly leaves poked her soft bottom.

'I was about to say, be careful of your bottom on my spiky top!' said Pip. 'Sorry!'

Lucky and Pip chuckled. The little cloud filled up with big, fluffy happiness and floated

at a safe distance above the pineapple's head,
joining in the adventure.

'Now turn right!' called Sammy.

Lucky leaned to the right. She only just
managed to dodge a wobbly flock of jelly
flamingos.

'Whoa!' everyone shouted again.

Sammy directed Lucky over Vanilla Valley
– where they all breathed in deep and went
'MMMMM!' – and through a swarm of
bumble peas that swept and swooped in vast
clouds, searching for sugar-bean canes. They
then skirted the coastline, where a hug whale
was bobbing below in the sea. Lucky slowed
down overhead and they called out, 'Hug us,

hug us!' and the hug whale blew them one of his very special hugs. It shot through his blowhole high in the air and covered them all in squidgy rainbow bubbles.

'This is the best trip ever,' Cami whooped, floofier than ever.

'I'm a bit hot, actually,' Pip panted.

'Oh! It's not the best trip ever if not everyone is happy,' Cami said. She grew a bit bigger and a little blue around the edges, and then covered Pip in a cool ice shower. 'Is that better?'

The pineapple shivered happily. 'Cool as a pine-cumber!' she said, doing a quick celebratory somersault and accidentally kicking Sammy in the bottom. '*Definitely* the best trip ever.'

'And we're nearly there. Look,' Sammy said, rubbing his bottom with one hand and pointing to the horizon with the other.

'Where are we actually going?' Cami asked, her pretty voice like pattering rain. 'I never asked.'

'We're off to the Blossom Festival on the other side of Charm Glade,' said Lucky. 'We're all entering the Cuteness Competition. Isn't that exciting?'

There was a short silence. Lucky looked behind to see what the problem was. Sammy and Pip were looking up at Cami. The little cloud had shrunk to the size of a sad puddle.

'But you *can't* enter the Cuteness Competition,' Cami said softly.

28

Lucky sensed a lot of unhappiness in the little cloud's voice. She came down to land on the top of a hill.

'Why, Cami?' she asked as the cloud floated to the ground as well. 'Whatever's the matter?'

'As I was passing over a dingly dell the other day, I overheard Clive the chihuahua talking to his friends, the Glamour Gang,' said Cami. 'He was saying that no one who had a tutu with fewer than fifteen layers of sparkle-net would *dare* enter the Cuteness Competition.'

Lucky looked at her friends. Pip had cool accessories. Cami was a *very* special cloud. She had a magical horn. All of them had brilliant cute-worthy talents . . . But not one of them had a tutu, let alone a tutu with fifteen layers of sparkle-net. Her heart sank.

'Oh no! I feel terrible,' she said. 'I persuaded you all to join me and for nothing!'

Pip triple-flipped into the air and on to the ground, Cami rained a little bit, and Sammy began scratching his –

'Oi! Who dares wake Tom-Tom?'

Pip's triple-flip had disturbed another sushi-mouse, curled up in a nearby tulip.

'I'm so sorry, Tom-Tom,' Pip said, peering at the little creature. 'Are you related to Dylan?'

Tom-Tom nodded grumpily. 'He's my hundred-and-fifth cousin, twice removed. We go for a roll together sometimes, but that's not important right now. What's important is–'

'Sleep?' yawned Sammy.

'No. What's important is your *attitude*.' Tom-Tom uncurled himself and stood on his little legs. He shook his tiny fists in the air. 'First you wake me up, which shows me you have no respect. Then you say you won't enter the

Cuteness Competition because of a chihuahua's tutu, which shows me you are wearing scaredy-pants.'

'I'm not wearing *any* pants,' Pip said, looking puzzled. 'No point. I keep making holes in them.'

Tom-Tom's tiny voice got bigger and bigger. 'Now, you cute lot, are you going to listen to the petty woofs of a selfish little dog? Or are you going to pull up your brave pants, put on your cutest acts and face that competition?'

The friends looked at each other and felt their hearts swell. Without having to say a word, they all agreed that they would go to the Blossom Festival and do their best and let the sushi-mouse go back to sleep.

'Thank you, sushi-mouse,' Lucky said.

'Go away, I'm sleeping,' said Tom-Tom.

'A sushi-mouse can sleep twenty-two and a half hours a day,' Sammy informed them.

'Not if you keep waking me up, I can't,' Tom-Tom grumbled.

They tiptoed away from Tom-Tom, who slammed the petals of his tulip shut and started mumbling himself back to sleep.

'That's decided,' Lucky said. 'We're all

entering the competition. A tutu is just a frilly skirt. And who need frills when you've got natural cuteness?'

Lucky tossed her mane. Sammy proudly flashed all the colours of the rainbow and Pip cartwheeled down the hill and backflipped back up again.

The triumphant moment was interrupted by a steady splatter of rain on their heads. Cami was suddenly crumpled and dark grey, like a gloomy tissue. Large water droplets were rolling down her cheeks.

'What's the matter, Cami?' Lucky asked.

'I'm just a boring little cloud,' Cami sobbed. The rain of tears got heavier and Lucky spread out her wings so Pip and Sammy could stay dry underneath. 'There's nothing cute about me.'

'We think you're the cutest cloud we've ever seen, don't we?' Lucky said.

'Yes!' Pip said, nodding. 'And you're brave, too. I've accidentally prickled you in the bottom at least twelve times and you haven't cried once.'

'As it happens,' Sammy said, 'I have a gap in my knowledge when it comes to clouds. Would you do me the pleasure of explaining what you can do?'

Cami gulped and turned a lighter shade of grey. 'Well . . .' she said. 'As you've seen, I can change shape. Light and fluffy when there's sun, blue and spiky when there's snow or ice, and grey when there's rain.'

'That's **SO COOOOOOL!**' Lucky said with a grin.

'But there's more,' Cami said, brightening up. She ploofed into a wide white cloud. 'I can rain anything I want. Here, give me a squeeze!'

Sammy reached up and squeezed a handful of Cami's cloudiness. She giggled and out popped miniature animals – octopuses, sharks, cows, chickens . . . They clucked, mooed and snuffled in the air before popping with little squeals of happiness, leaving tiny multi-coloured wisps which drifted away into the sky.

'That's incredible!' Pip said, leaping to catch a tiny kangaroo before it popped.

Cami gave a shy smile. 'Sometimes, when I get lonely, I make myself little friends like these. They don't stick around long, though. After a while, they tend to . . . pop off.'

'Well, we're your friends and we're definitely sticking around, Cami,' Lucky said.

'Really?' Cami lit up and showered them with mini-furniture – tiny chairs, tables, beds and lamps. She giggled. 'Oops, I don't know why I did that!'

'That's a really cute act, Cami!' said Lucky. 'You have *got* to see if you can enter the competition! The World of Cute needs to see your super skills!'

But hiding in the bushes, watching and

listening, was the Glamour Gang.

They didn't like what they were seeing and hearing. And they were making decidedly un-cute plans . . .

CHAPTER THREE

The Blossom Festival

The friends continued their journey through the bright blue sky, full of smiles and good feelings. They had each other and they had some super cute talents to show off. Or . . . did they?

'Lucky,' Pip said. 'We know you can fly – and great flying, by the way –'

'Great flying!' the others agreed.

'But what's your *cute* talent?' Pip asked.

'Well . . .' Lucky ducked beneath a cloud of bright lumi-bugs, '. . . my horn glows by the light of the moon! It happened for the first time last night.'

'Oooh!' went her friends.

'That's triple-fliptastic, Lucky!' Pip declared.

'Stormingly brilliant!' Cami whooped.

Sammy cleared his throat. 'There's a bit of a problem with that,' he said. 'The Blossom Festival is a daytime event and the moon won't be out. So there's a very good chance your horn won't light up.'

Lucky gave a little kick with her back legs, making everyone bounce on her back.

'Oh, that's OK!' she said cheerfully. 'Now my horn has lit up for the first time, it's ready to do its next magic trick.'

'What's the trick?' Cami said, bouncing in the air with excitement.

'Actually, I have no idea.' Lucky paused.

'But I THINK it'll be something very cute. My sister's horn makes everyone dance, and my mum's horn can make the stars in the sky form any shape she wants.'

'That's as cool as pineapples in fridges dressed as cucumbers!' shouted Pip.

'But how do you make it happen?' Sammy asked, pushing his glasses up his nose. 'Do you twist your horn? Do you flap your wings? How do you know it will happen when you want it to?'

'I'm not sure,' said Lucky. 'My mum says it'll happen when the time is right. Maybe I just have to think hard.' She thought hard. 'Or sneeze.' She sneezed. 'ATCHOO!

Or sing.' She sang. 'LA LA LA! Oh dear . . .'

Suddenly, Lucky felt very scared indeed. She didn't know HOW to make the magic happen. How would she do it in the Cuteness Competition?

'Like your mum said, it'll happen when the time is right,' Cami soothed. 'And there's no better time than the Cuteness Competition. I'm sure everything will be fine.'

'Of course it will,' Pip said. 'And we'll be here for you, whatever happens.'

'Absolutely,' Sammy said. 'Positive thinking is a very powerful tool. Studies have shown that people who have a positive mental attitude are far more likely to succeed when they –'

'Everyone, we're here!' Cami interrupted. 'I can see the tents.'

'Oh my goodness, we're here, we're here! I'm so excited!' Pip leaped up and bumped her spikes on Cami's bottom.

'OUCH!' squeaked Cami.

Lucky gave a shake of her mane, hoping to shake off her worries. Her friends were right. She just needed to think positively. 'I'd better land before there are any more accidents!' she said.

'Good, because I've got an itch coming,' Sammy said. 'Very hard to scratch yourself when on top of a flying lunacorn. I can't quite reach my –'

'Hold on!' Lucky stretched out her wings and they glided down to the grass plain.

They weren't alone. There were gaggles of flavour-crayons, cowboy fridges, candyfloss cacti, and milkshakes frothing with excitement.

Cuties of all shapes and sizes were making their way towards the tents, wearing brilliant costumes and flower garlands. The air was thick with the smell of candied nuts and it made the friends' tummies rumble.

The blare of music bands and happy whistles excited them even more.

'Come on, this way!' Pip shouted, tumbling like an acrobat towards the tents.

'Don't wear yourself out,' Lucky warned. 'Just walk with us – oooh, that's strange.'

They were passing a large sign which said:

'It's been changed,' said Lucky. 'Look, the original words were *Love Life, Be Cute*.'

'And this one!' Pip gasped. 'It originally said *Cuteness 4 Ever.* But now it says *Cuteness 4 The Winner.*'

A flurry of snowflakes fell from Cami. 'That's not really in the Blossom Festival spirit,' she said sadly.

'I don't want to alarm you,' Sammy said, 'but read this one. I think someone is trying to make a point.'

A sign saying *You're All Too Cute* had been changed to *Clive's Tutu Cute.*

'This has got something to do with the Glamour Gang,' Cami said with a frown. 'I'm sure of it.'

Their conversation was drowned out by

the loud **PA—PAARP** of a marching cupcake band. The tunes from a cupcake band were so lovely they could usually turn any sour moment into absolute sweetness. But nothing could cover up the bad taste of the vandalised signs and the feeling that something wasn't right.

A trombonist lowered her instrument as she passed the gang. '**PSSST!** Listen up,' she said. 'A dog did this. A little ratty one. I saw him earlier. It makes me angry. The Cuteness Competition should be a time for fun . . .' The cupcake shook her head so hard that some sprinkles fell off. Then she scurried to catch up with her band.

'Clive,' Pip said sternly. 'What a little rot-dog.'

Lucky didn't like to be mean. She'd never even met Clive. 'Maybe he's just overexcited about being cute. Dogs do get that way,' she said.

Cami turned a worried shade of grey. 'I hope you're right.'

'Let's give him a chance,' Pip agreed.

☆ ☆ ☆

They quickly forgot about the strange signs as their eyes sparkled with the fun of the fair. Face-painters decorated partygoers with glitter swirls, candy cones blew sugar mist in the air while artists twisted bubblegums into animal shapes. Lucky spotted a funny bunny holding a funny-bunny balloon, and it was hard to tell which was which.

'Look, there's a dog agility contest!' Pip said, backflipping on the spot with excitement.

The pineapple set off, running alongside the dogs and copying their moves as they leaped and slalomed between lollypop posts. The dogs were dressed in ribbons and bows and had brightly dyed fur. A group of happy woofers formed a pyramid, standing on each other's shoulders. Lucky gasped as she saw the spiky little pineapple run, tumble and leap into the top spot. 'Ta-da!'

'**BRAVO, PIP!**' she called.

Lucky's attention was suddenly caught by an incessant barking at the edge of the stage.

A little dog who looked a bit like a furry rat was yapping at the agility judge. The judge nervously took a rosette off a lovable hot dog, who was drooping with sadness, and pinned it on to the collar of the yappy dog.

Cami floated closer to Lucky. 'That's Clive,'

she whispered. 'He just stole the prize from Weener.'

Lucky's jaw dropped. She couldn't believe it!

Now a strange assortment of characters was running towards Clive, showering him with praise.

'Bravo!'

'Best dog in show!'

'World class!'

This must be the Glamour Gang! Lucky could see a pizza slice, an angry muffin, a snail and a scooter. And every single one of them was wearing a TUTU!

'Tutus were first worn hundreds of years ago in a performance at the opera,' Sammy began. 'They were originally made of a kind of netting called gauze, which was designed to . . .'

As Sammy chatted about the history of the tutu, Lucky stared at the Glamour Gang with an uneasy feeling in her tummy. It did seem that the little chihuahua would do *anything* to win. Noodle-ifying, cake-ifying and now *stealing*. How were they going to compete against someone so mean?

And with all this worry, would she ever find the power to work her magic horn?

CHAPTER FOUR

Backstage Drama!

The Cuteness Competition tent was pitched in the centre of the fair. There was a large stage covered in a wide rainbow canvas. A colourful, glittery sign hung above it.

SUPER CUTE
Just Be You!

The grassy area in front of the platform was filling up fast with spectators, all chatting excitedly about the contestants and who they thought might win. Bunting fluttered and the cupcake band marched up and down, blowing delicious cake smells and music from their instruments. Red apple usherettes roller-skated between the rows, handing out jellybeans.

Lucky and her friends watched it all with wide eyes.

'We'll just do our best,' Lucky said, feeling a bit nervous as she sniffed the sweet music that floated by. 'That's all anyone can ask for, and it's all we can do.'

'Right,' said Cami, shedding a few drops of rain. She took a jellybean pouch and poured every single last jellybean into her mouth. 'Right,' she said again.

'Let's do it,' said Pip, jumping up – and tripping over Sammy who had fallen asleep at her feet. 'Sammy!'

The sloth turned red with embarrassment. 'What? Oh, is it time?'

The changing-room entrance was at the side of the tent. Contestants were streaming in and out like fancy ants. Some of them *were* fancy ants.

'Read this!' Lucky said. She pointed to a sign on a stick.

RULES

ENTRANTS ARE ENCOURAGED TO PERFORM THEIR NATURAL TALENTS.

DISPLAY YOUR SKILLS AND YOUR GIFTS.

SHOW US HOW YOU WERE BORN TO BE CUTE!

Cami started to wobble. 'I'm scared,' she whispered.

'Don't worry, Cami,' said Lucky. 'Remember the stage sign, Super Cute – *Just Be You!*'

'Ahem. Ahem. *Ahem.*'

The friends turned to see a little carrot holding a clipboard. The carrot was clearing his throat in a determined way. He flicked aside his mane of long green leaves and opened his hand in front of them.

'Invites, please,' he said firmly.

Lucky rummaged in her backpack and produced her slightly scrumpled invite. The carrot checked the list on his clipboard and handed it back.

'And the others?' he asked, looking at Cami, Pip and Sammy.

'My friends don't have invitations,' Lucky said. 'And Sammy here doesn't want to enter. But my friends Pip and Cami do, and two extra acts won't take much time! And it's such a lovely day . . .' She gave him her best smile.

The carrot frowned.

'There won't be any fuss, I promise!' Lucky said. She thought of the stage sign. 'We don't have any props or dancing troops of funny bunnies. They've come to *just be them*. Like it says on the sign.'

The carrot looked at Pip. The pineapple did a hopeful backflip, losing her goggles in mid-air. Then the carrot raised his eyes to Cami, who dropped a tiny bear on his head. He smiled.

'Well, I do like the look of you both,' he said. 'But the line-up is full, and I –'

He was interrupted by a little bok-choy, tugging at his clipboard.

'What is it, Bart?' said the carrot. 'Pardon? What? You've lost your voice? Oh dear, you can't sing Cabbaggio's Operetta for Greens with no voice. I *am* sorry. We'll have to make sure you get an invitation next year.'

'So!' The carrot turned back to Lucky and her pals. 'It seems we do have ONE space. The funny pineapple can enter!'

Pip put her goggles back on her face and peeped out at the carrot. 'Thank you,' she said. 'I'm really grateful. I am. But I don't want to enter without my friend, Cami.'

'I see . . .' The carrot thought for a moment, paced three steps back, muttered something they couldn't hear, and paced three steps forward again.

'Well,' he said. 'I've just had a word with myself and apparently I believe that sometimes we need to do the right thing. As a competition official I can make special allowances and

I declare that Cami the cloud is allowed to enter. So there.'

He gave a happy sigh, scribbled down their names on his list, slapped gold name badges on them all and waved them into the tent with a flick of a green frond. Lucky, Pip and Cami thanked the carrot – but when they went backstage and saw the rest of the performers, they stopped in their tracks and stared.

The air was full of song and dance. There were trapezing pom-poms and hula-hooping avocados . . . It was like a circus of talent all in one room.

Cami hovered closer to Lucky. 'I'm not sure

I can do this,' she said. 'Everyone is so brilliant.'

'And so are *you*,' Lucky said reassuringly. 'Come on, let's meet some people. When you see they're like you and me, you won't be so scared. Hi, who are you?' she said to a large golden dog with oodles of poodle fur and a glowing nose.

'I'm Louis the labradoodle,' said the dog. 'My talent is painting with my nose.'

'That's great!' Lucky said.

'I'm Dee the dumpling kitty,' mewed a furball at their feet. 'EXCUUUUUSE ME!'

Dee rolled across the room through the legs of all the contestants. When she got to the refreshments table, several cakes quickly vanished into her mouth and a few more disappeared into her bag.

'I wonder what her talent is?' Pip said. 'Rolling? Cake making? Cake eating?'

'The biggest ever cake-eating competition was won by a woodland dolphin named Petal, who ate two hundred and fifty cakes in one sitting.' Sammy said. His fur turned green at the thought of it.

Lucky had started to feel a bit queasy too. Everyone seemed so sure of their act. What if she stood on stage in front of all these cuties and . . . nothing happened? Her horn would do something cute, *when the time was right.* That's what her mum had said. But what if this wasn't the right time? Was she silly to think her magic would appear so soon? To make things worse, she didn't have a back-up plan. With the sun out, she couldn't even make her horn GLOW!

'Look!' Pip pointed at a chihuahua wearing a cape pinned with a rosette. The little dog was sitting in a basket on the handlebars of a scooter.

'It's Clive!' Cami gasped. 'And the scooter is part of the Glamour Gang!'

Clive rode round the costume racks and work stations, checking out the talents and watching the rehearsals.

'Not good enough,' he snapped, pointing at Louis the labradoodle's nose-sketch of a hippopotamus.

'Footwork's atrocious!' he barked at a tap-dancing owl.

'Did you even *think* about your outfit for *one* second?' he gasped, pointing at a giant pink hamster wearing a walnut whip.

Pip leaped on to Lucky's back and whispered in her ear, 'He's trying to put them off their rehearsals.'

Lucky agreed with Pip. At first, she had thought Clive was trying to help them improve their acts, but he wasn't making helpful suggestions at all. He was trying to destroy their confidence.

'I'm sure that they just need to go out on stage and be themselves,' she said. 'That's what I'm going to do. I *hope* . . .'

Clive snapped his head round sharply.

'Take me to the lunacorn!' he ordered the scooter.

The scooter did as it was told.

Clive twitched his pointy nose at Lucky. His eyes narrowed and his voice twisted to a high-pitched growl. 'I don't know WHO you think you are, but perfect cuteness is not achieved overnight,' he yipped. 'It is achieved through hard work, or, if you're like me, through breeding. I come from a long line of royal cuteness. Pedigree stock. My father was Duke Pawston, my grandfather was Fredrik Furdeville, my great-grandmother – Lady Pratterly-Lick. All of them winners. **WINNERS!**' he shouted.

The whole room had stopped talking and was looking at Clive. It was a chance for the

chihuahua to make himself crystal clear.

'Not one of you has got what it takes,' Clive hissed, eyeballing every single cutie in the tent. 'You're all LOSERS!'

The scooter spun round and Clive motored away.

The changing room slowly came back to life. But it wasn't happy and chatty like before. There were murmurs and mumbles. A few sobs. Many contestants packed up their things and left. Dee the dumpling kitty shared her cakes with them all as they left the tent, trying to cheer them up.

Lucky felt her heart drop. She was sad for all of the contestants who had decided they weren't good enough because of what Clive had said. And she was also a little worried that she, Lucky the lunacorn, had got it all wrong. Perhaps it wasn't enough to *just be you* after all.

She wondered if she should go, too.

But it was too late. The cupcake band had started up again and the tootle horns were blowing. The Cuteness Competition was about to begin!

CHAPTER FIVE

Floods of Kindness

'Everybody, everybody!' said a voice over the loudspeaker. It boomed like an elephant's trumpet, although it came from a rather small, smartly-dressed mushroom holding a microphone. 'It is time for the cuteness to commence!'

The crowd cheered. The mushroom looked down at his list.

'This year's contest will not be in order of height like last year, but in order of the alphabet,' said the mushroom. 'So please, put your hands together for our first contestant . . . Cami the cloud, to be followed by Clive the chihuahua!'

The cheers were so loud that they bounced off the roof of the tent. In the wings, Cami stared at her friends with big frightened eyes.

'Go on, you'll be brilliant,' said Lucky, giving Cami a little nudge.

Cami floated on and hovered above the

stage. A drop of nervous rain pattered on the wooden boards below.

'Oh no! She's going to rain!' someone shouted.

'Come on, Cami,' Sammy whispered loudly. 'You can do it!'

Cami looked at her friends. Their smiles were like sunshine. She smiled back. Then she popped into a puffball cloud, fluffier than whipped marshmallow. The crowd went 'AAAH!', then 'OOOH!' as she turned wintery-blue and spiky like a floating crystal. Then she made them shriek with her thundery look: dark grey with a pulse of maroon, as if she had lightning in her tummy. Then she stopped as if she had completely forgotten what to do!

Sammy spotted the problem. He rolled towards Cami, camouflaging himself against the wooden stage, and gave her a big comforting squeeze.

Cami sighed with relief. A shower of fluffy ducklings rained down over the audience, making everyone gasp, *'That's so cute!'* before the ducklings quacked, squealed and popped into thin air. When the duckling rain stopped, the crowd clapped like crazy. BRILLIANT!

'And now, for more special rain!' Cami said, filling out with confidence. She nodded for Sammy to squeeze her again. 'A shower of sherbet elephants!'

But as Sammy stepped forward to give her another squeeze, two members of the Glamour Gang gripped his arms and legs and dragged him off the stage.

Clive gave a mean-lipped smile. Cami hovered nervously, waiting for her sloth friend to come back. She tried to squeeze herself, but it wasn't working. Lucky could see that her cloud friend was getting more and more upset until . . . Cami turned dark blue with disappointment and flooded the stage with her tears.

The judging panel muttered and scribbled in their notepads. Cami whirled offstage in a tornado of worry and shame.

'Don't worry,' Lucky said, pulling the little cloud in for a soggy hug. 'We thought you were amazing.'

'Clive and his gang ruined it,' Pip said crossly. 'I'll go and find Sammy. Those rascals dragged him outside.'

She returned a minute later, hand in hand with the sloth, whose spectacles were wonky. He was looking slightly dazed.

'How did you get Sammy back?' Cami asked, sniffing.

'I just air-cartwheeled towards the Glamour Gang. It's a basic pine-ninja move.' Pip gave a wink. '*Unfortunately*, my spiky leaves popped out and poked them in the bottoms. So they ran away.'

'You're brilliant, Pip,' Lucky said, glad they were all back together. 'Now gather round. I've got an idea.'

Sammy, Pip and Cami huddled close to Lucky.

'Clive knows that people don't like him and he's used to people being mean about him,' said Lucky. 'So maybe that's why he's so mean back. Perhaps if we showered him with kindness, it will give him an opportunity to show everyone his nicer side?'

'Kindness can never hurt,' Cami said. 'But how can we be kind in the middle of a competition?'

Lucky tapped her hoof as she thought about it. 'I know,' she said. 'He's on next, so why don't we clean the stage for him? A dog as cute as Clive should have a sparkling stage for his act, right?'

'Right!' said Pip.

'And I know how to do it!' Cami said. She puffed herself up, bigger and bigger until she looked like a giant pillow. 'Come on, Sammy. We've got some cleaning to do!'

Cami scooted low across the stage, absorbing the puddles of water she had left behind. Sammi rolled behind her, his fur acting just like a mop. Within seconds, the stage was shiny and new, the perfect platform for a

superstar. Everyone cheered and laughed as Sammy and Cami squeezed themselves out over the grass next to the tent.

Clive did not join in the cheer. He stood at the side of the stage, fluffing out his fifteen-layer tutu and muttering how his costume designer should have added more.

The well-dressed mushroom came back on. 'And now, for our second contestant tonight . . . Our two-time winner . . . Clive the chihuahua!'

The tent fell silent. A single bright spotlight flicked on, illuminating Clive in his outrageous tutu. He threw back his head, fluttered his eyelashes and struck a pose with one paw high in the air and one back leg stretched out behind. They audience held its breath. This was Clive's attempt at winning the Cuteness Competition *three times in a row*. He was bound to do something spectacular. What would it be? Whisker twanging? Balancing on a beach ball? A tutu trapeze act?

The music began. Clive cleared his throat.

'He's going to sing!' Lucky whispered to her friends.

But what would the pedigree cuteness winner warble? An opera – *Tutu fan Frutti*? A film soundtrack – *The Sound of Tutus*? A song cover – *You're Tutu Shy*? Or something original?

A lonely trumpet note dangled in the air – the cue for Clive to begin. He opened his muzzle and . . . out came . . .

A **YOWL** that sounded like glass smashing.

Everyone covered their ears. But it only got worse. The chihuahua's shaky little voice **WHINED** like a thousand angry wasps and **GROANED** like a bear with a tummy ache.

No one knew *what* Clive was singing. Or if it was *singing* at all!

Clive strutted around the stage, twirling and flouncing and fluffing out his tutu. As he continued to screech his song, he kept pointing to his tutu, as if fifteen layers of sparkle-net alone would win the prize. But the judges had dropped their notepads and were staring with disbelief. Even the Glamour Gang had their paws, pastry and handlebars over their ears. But as Clive's musical number came to an end, they became his adoring fans once again.

'You were incredible!'

'What talent!'

'You blew them away!'

Clive trotted off the stage with his nose high. He turned to wave at his fans before disappearing behind the curtain. The poor little pooch had no idea how bad he was!

Some of the contestants grinned at each other, pleased at Clive's disastrous act. But Lucky felt sorry for the chihuahua. Surely all the pedigree breeding (and cheating) in the world wasn't going to win him the Cuteness Competition this year. And it wasn't nice to laugh because someone was having a bad day. Even if that someone was mean.

Lucky was suddenly struck by a terrible thought. Perhaps soon they would be laughing at *her*. Without knowing how to make her magic

work, how could she be sure this wouldn't be a
bad day for her too?

CHAPTER SIX

Talents and Tantrums!

Next on the stage was Dee the dumpling kitty. Lucky cheered loudly. She was looking forward to seeing Dee's special skill.

Dee rolled on to the stage and raised her paws in the air. The crowd drummed their feet in anticipation.

The dumpling kitty stuck her hands into her fur and brought out blocks of play-dough. Within seconds she had built incredible sculptures of fairy houses, drumsticks and a full set of drums.

'She's amazing!' Pip said.

'So creative,' Cami agreed.

Dee started pulling out flowers and arranging them into bouquets in mid-air, and lengths of material that she magically snipped and sewed into accessories: a handbag, a hat, a scarf. The crowd cried 'AAAH!' and clapped enthusiastically. But the marvellous mood was disturbed by a sudden cry of rage from offstage. A yap that demanded attention.

'Disqualified! Not allowed!'

Clive marched on to the stage, still wearing his fifteen-layer tutu. He picked up a sequinned dress Dee had made and tossed it off the stage. He kicked down her play-dough sculptures and stamped on the bouquets. When there was nothing left to destroy, he pointed accusingly at Dee. The dumpling kitty and her fur fluffed up crossly. She didn't mind dogs, but she wasn't keen on ones that barked in her face!

'No props!' Clive shouted, pointing at the debris. 'It's not *natural*!'

Lucky shook her head. She had been happy to give Clive a chance, but now he'd ruined Dee's show, she couldn't stand by and say nothing.

She stepped on to the stage. 'If Dee's clay is a prop,' she said, 'then so is your tutu!'

Clive bared his teeth and did a peculiar little shuffle at Lucky's feet. He gave a long, shrill growl that rattled like a baby's toy, and then stamped on her hooves. Lucky stumbled backwards in shock – and fell off the stage!

'Tell it to the paw, because this CUTE face isn't listening!' Clive barked down at her.

Lucky had landed on the grass in front of the stage with all four hooves in the air, beside Clive's entourage in the front row. The Glamour Gang pizza slice stepped forward. For a moment, Lucky thought it was going to offer her help. But she should have known better. This was the Glamour Gang after all.

'Leave Clive alone!' the pizza screamed.

'He's trained all year for this! It's *his* show!'

Lucky got to her feet as her friends arrived. She wasn't hurt, but she was furious! Cami showered soothing remedy petals and stroked the lunacorn's ears with her cloud fluff, but Lucky was too upset to calm down.

'Forget him, Lucky,' Sammy said. 'I told you from the beginning he was a bad egg. Everyone at the contest is just doing their best, and he has to ruin it for everyone with his little tantrums!'

Lucky sighed. 'I know,' she said. 'But it's not Clive I'm worried about. It's me. Here I am, planning to go onstage . . . but I don't even know what I'm doing yet. Or if I can do *anything*!'

Pip gave her friend a quick prickle on the chin.

'OUCH!' said Luna. 'Be careful, Pip!'

'I did that one on purpose!' cried Pip. 'Snap out of it, Lucky. Remember – *just be you*. And *you* shine wherever you go. Wait and see. You'll be dazzling.'

The smart little mushroom waddled back on to the stage.

'Our next contestant is . . . Connor the cannoli!' he announced.

The crowd cheered and clapped as a cream-filled cannoli took to the stage and launched into a very energetic dance routine.

'I've seen the list and there are a few more

acts before you,' Pip told Lucky. 'I just spotted Hannah the hairbrush. She has so many bristles, her act will take ages. Try to relax and enjoy the show. We'll be back in a minute.'

'Wait! Where are you going?' Lucky asked.

But her friends had already vanished into the crowds.

Lucky tried to have fun. But all the acts were so brilliant that it only made her more nervous. And her friends were taking ages to come back. Where were they and what were they doing?

'Lucky the lunacorn!'

'What?' Lucky looked at the stage in terror.

The mushroom was beckoning. 'Come on, Lucky. I can see you out there . . . Cuties, please put your hands together and welcome Lucky to the stage!'

'Me?' Lucky gasped. 'It's me *already*?'

Her friends were still nowhere to be seen. She was all alone. Shaking so much that her wings wobbled, Lucky made her way to the stage. The crowd fell silent. Even Clive and the Glamour Gang were ominously quiet. Lucky felt as if the whole world had stopped to watch her show, and now she was going to let them all down.

She smiled nervously. 'My act today is . . .'

'Get on with it!' shouted a strange voice, which sounded like a high-pitched chihuahua putting on a deep voice.

Lucky looked around in despair. 'Okay,' she stammered. 'I'm going to . . .'

There was a wave of noise from the crowd as a giant cloud blocked out the sun above, plunging the stage into darkness.

'Cami? Is that you?' Lucky whispered.

She suddenly saw Pip slipping on to the stage through the back curtains, followed by a group of silver-foil flitterlings. And Sammy!

He was busy ushering in swarms of glow-bugs and lumi-flies.

'What are you guys doing?' Lucky asked helplessly.

The swarms drifted to the roof of the tent and came together in a ball above Lucky's head. The million little lights of the glow-bugs and lumi-flies reflected off the silver wings of the flitterlings and . . . they *shone*.

Lucky laughed with delight. Her friends had created a night sky and a *moon*!

 As the moonlight fell across her face, her horn began to glow. It was working! It was working! The brighter it glowed, the happier Lucky became.

'MARVELLOUS!' cried the crowd. 'MAGNIFICENT!'

Lucky spread her wings and pranced around the stage. Suddenly her horn glowed blue, green and pink. She didn't know it did rainbow colours too!

She looked up to see Cami smiling above her. Then she looked to the right at Pip and to the left at Sammy, who had turned a happy shade of orange. Her heart filled with love. What wonderful, wonderful friends!

Suddenly, like a giant fountain, a great cloud of butterfly confetti sprayed from the top of Lucky's horn. The pretty party papers floated to the floor.

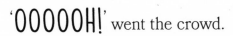

'OOOOOH!' went the crowd.

Lucky's horn glowed brighter and brighter. It started to fizz and crackle like a dazzling bonfire sparkler. Now she felt her wings tingle and magically grow. She stretched them out so they spanned the width of the stage and began to beat them up and down.

> POP!! <

Streamers and candies exploded from her horn and shot into the air! There were cries of happiness and yumminess as the sweeties started to show their own special magic. They turned into whatever flavour you loved the best! Watermelon, peanut butter, marshmallow s'mores . . . anything you could dream of!

Lucky flew around the stage in joy. Everyone cheered and clapped and whooped like never before. Well, everyone apart from Clive and the Glamour Gang, who jumped up and down trying to grab all the sweets so that nobody else could enjoy them.

When Lucky saw this, she felt very cross. Suddenly her horn glowed green and some dragon-shaped candies flew out. They swooped down to Clive and his mean pals, and chased them out of the tent in a cloud of multi-coloured magic!

'YIP!' howled Clive.

'YOW!' screeched the Glamour Gang.

Now everyone could enjoy the show.

And the treats!

'You're amazing!' the crowd shouted. 'Truly super cute!'

Lucky swooped past Cami. 'Thank you,' she whispered.

Cami winked. 'You're welcome!'

Lucky came in to land. She pulled Sammy and Pip close. 'You did this,' she said.

'No, *you* did this!' Sammy and Pip replied.

Lucky smiled. '*Friendship* did this.'

There were cries of 'MORE! MORE!' from the audience. Lucky tossed her head and fired one last fountain of sweets from her horn. They fell around the crowd like they were falling through honey.

'Slow-motion treats!' everyone cheered.

Everyone reached up to snatch the slow-moving sweets from the air. There were cries of delight as the candies exploded on their tongues in lip-smacking flavours.

Then the glow-bugs, lumi-flies and flitterlings drifted away, and the light in Lucky's horn faded. Everyone in the audience was still cheering, but was it enough?

Lucky glanced at the judges. They were on their feet, clapping. She breathed a massive happy sigh. She could finally relax. She had done her best, her absolute cutest. She'd done what she was born to do.

A screeching yap cut through the air.

'Cheat!'

'Disqualified!'

'She used props!'

It was Clive and the mean Glamour Gang, shouting through the door of the tent. But, for once, no one paid them the slightest bit of attention!

CHAPTER SEVEN

And the Winner is . . .

A little while later, all the contestants had performed. Pip's pine-ninja display hadn't *quite* gone to plan – she'd slipped on a candy wrapper and landed in the audience during an ambitious triple side spin – but the audience had LOVED it. They'd carried her through the air chanting her name and Pip had enjoyed every minute!

But now it was time to announce the winner.

All of the contestants stood on stage and waited for the judges' decision. Even though it was a competition, it felt more like a team effort and there was lots of hugging.

Dee the dumpling kitty made everyone a winner's medal. Pip kept the crowd entertained with a spectacular pine-ninja dancing display while the judges talked things over. Sammy made young members of the audience laugh by turning himself all sorts of interesting colours. He was in the middle of being rhubarb when the little mushroom marched on to the stage.

The mushroom stood in front of the contestants and looked out at the spectators. Everyone hushed and wriggled with anticipation.

'The judges have arrived at their decision,' he said. 'It was very tough with so many excellent acts, but this year's Cuteness Competition Winner title is awarded to . . .' He stopped as a judge handed him a piece of paper. 'Oh, goodness,' he said in surprise. 'This has never happened before in the history of the competition, but there are *two* winners. Cami the cloud AND Lucky the lunacorn!'

Lucky and Cami looked at each other with shock and delight. The others rushed to wrap them in hugs and kisses and they all jumped up and down with excitement.

'Both acts were full of cuteness, kindness . . . and surprises!' continued the mushroom.

'We were very impressed with how Cami overcame her shyness to perform. We also liked how she helped her friend, Lucky. It was an extraordinary display of friendship. And we all hugely enjoyed Lucky's performance. The candies were really extraordinary!'

The little mushroom glanced at the grumbling Glamour Gang, still hanging around outside the tent. Then he winked at Lucky, who blushed. 'So, everyone,' he said. 'Without further ado, let's congratulate our winners!'

Lucky and Cami ducked down so that a cactus assistant could place winner sashes over their heads and shoulders. The cactus gave them each a kiss on the cheek. It prickled a bit,

but they were getting pretty used to it with Pip's spiky hugs, and both were too happy to care.

The mushroom tapped his microphone. 'Enjoy the rest of the Blossom Festival,' he said with a smile. 'And don't forget, dear friends – you are ALL super cute!'

The whole tent erupted in joy. Everyone

linked arms, wings and other things, and sang, *'For They Are Jolly Cute Cuties and So Say All of Us!'*

Clive's furious barking could be heard above it all.

'This is preposterous!' he yelled from outside. 'You can't win by . . . being *friends*. Competitions aren't supposed to be *friendly*. Total rot. Ridiculous. What about the training, the *breeding*? I'm from a long, important line of pedigree cuteness, you know!'

But no one was in the mood for listening to a sore loser.

While Lucky's heart was bursting with happiness for herself and her friends, she felt a bit sad for Clive. Surely, all he needed was a big friendly hug, and to be told by friends – *real* friends – that he didn't need to prove himself to anyone. He was a splendid little chihuahua with a flair for drama and style. The Glamour Gang should have been telling him that all along, instead of praising him for something he wasn't. The truth was, Clive the chihuahua was *not* a natural singer.

When the excitement had died down, Lucky and her friends moved away from the noise to celebrate with a quiet picnic at the edge of Charm Glade. They invited Dee the dumpling kitty along too. The poor thing was still a little bit shaken from Clive's attack, but when she realised she was among true friends she relaxed. She told her new friends that she could produce absolutely *anything* from her special bag or the deep pockets in her fur!

'I'm in the mood for a smoothie!' Dee said, pulling out five glasses of sweet berry smoothies from her fur. 'Isn't this the greatest day? What

a festival, what a party! What brilliant new friends. Thanks for letting me come along.'

'You're very welcome,' Lucky said. 'Friendship makes great things happen. So the more the merrier.'

Two squeaky voices suddenly piped up from a cluster of flowers behind them.

'Oi!'

'Yeah, oi!'

Dylan and Tom-Tom, the sushi-mice, were standing on the top of a large daisy. The flower swayed precariously under their weight.

'Oh no, we didn't wake you up again, did we?' Pip said.

'Not this time. I just came to say well done,' Dylan said.

'And I just wanted to say how proud I am that you took off your scaredy-pants and faced your fears,' said Tom-Tom.

Dylan yawned. 'We're going back to bed now.'

'I haven't had anywhere *near* my twenty-two and a half hours' sleep today,' Tom-Tom said. He looked pointedly at Sammy. 'So leave us alone. But well done.'

The two sushi-mice vanished back into the flowers.

The super cutes held in their giggles until they were certain the sushi-mice had gone. Then it came out in a burst of laughter so big that it made their tummies warm and their eyes water. It lasted so long that they thought they might never stop.

Laughing with their friends did funny things. Sammy's fur turned stripy like a candy cane, and Pip flipped so high that she managed four forward rolls and a double-twist. Cami showered down inflatable bath toys and they were all as happy as could be.

CHAPTER EIGHT

A Magical Night

The friends sat slurping their smoothies as hundreds of dipsy daisies and friendly flowers surrounded them and began to twirl around the field. They wafted flower-power perfume all around, which made everyone dizzy with happiness.

'The largest blossom at the festival is always the daisy gigantis,' Sammy said. 'Quite a remarkable flower, with an even number of petals. Sometimes pink, but most often white. The middle, however, is always, *always* cornflower blue. But my favourite blossom has to be the spinning lily – see how the star-shape twirls so beautifully? The Blossom Festival dance troop record is six hundred spinning lilies, and –'

'Have a cookie, Sammy, before your mouth gets tired!' Dee made an extra-large cookie appear from her fur.

The friends all hooted and hugged Sammy, who was blushing all over. 'I just can't help telling you facts!' he said apologetically.

'Well, we love everything you say and *that's* a fact!' Pip said.

The blossom dancers showered them with perfume and edible popping petals and pranced away. Then it was just the friends again, on the grass, feeling fine.

'This might have been the best day of my life,' Lucky said.

'Because you won the contest?' Pip asked, roly-polying towards her.

'No! Because of all of *you*,' said Lucky, laughing. 'You showed me that I'm at my best when I'm surrounded by friends and you helped me find my special talent. I would NEVER have guessed that my magic includes confetti and treats. The dragon candies were a particularly BIG surprise!'

Cami giggled. 'That was pretty cool!'

'It was!' said Pip, nodding. 'You showed Clive that he couldn't get away with his mean behaviour.' She lifted up her cool goggles. 'I had a LOT of fun today! Thank you for inviting me.'

'It was great. You all did brilliantly, just by being yourselves,' Lucky said with a smile.

'I was completely myself and fell asleep and missed most of the show,' Sammy confessed.

'I've got an interesting fact for you, Sammy,' Pip said with a grin. 'Did you know you scratch your bottom in your sleep?'

Sammy chuckled. 'I knew I had an unconscious itch.'

And they fell about laughing again.

'I don't know about you,' Dee said, rummaging in her bag, 'but I think this moment calls for cake.'

'Every moment calls for cake when you're around, Dee,' Lucky said.

'Yup! But this time it's special,' Dee replied, whipping out a cardboard box.

Inside the box was a sponge cake with lemon-cream icing. The words *Cute Friends Forever* was written across the top in green and red sugar-beads.

'There's one rule about this cake,' said Dee. 'Only SUPER cuties are allowed a slice. So who's super cute?'

'Me,' said Sammy. 'I'm feeling extremely cute.'

'Me, too,' said Pip.

'Me three,' Cami cried.

'Me four,' said Dee. 'What about you, Lucky?'

Lucky smiled bashfully. 'Well, yes. I must say, I am feeling cute. But . . .'

'But?' Cami said.

Lucky sighed. 'I feel sorry for Clive. I don't suppose he is feeling cute right now. I hope that one day he'll work out what he needs to do.'

'He will,' Cami reassured her. 'But until that day, I hope I never bump into that competitive little chihuahua again!'

'Being who you are always wins the day,' Pip said.

Lucky smiled. 'Being with your friends always *makes* your day.'

They all high-fived and scoffed Dee's incredible cute cake.

☆ ☆ ☆

When the afternoon turned to evening, they packed up and walked back towards the festival to see Moloko the milk carton's Clowns and Cookies Circus Show. Fairy lights were twinkling. The marching cake band had reformed into smaller jelly jazz bands, which played music so soothing that it made you wobble if you didn't sit down among the blossoms covering the ground.

The slowly darkening sky was lit by glow-bugs and lumi-flies, who all had a great story to take home to their friends about helping

a lunacorn win the Cuteness Competition.

'Hello! Hello, Lucky!' they called in their tiny voices, and Lucky blew them kisses which made them spin and tumble in the air.

As the friends sat together, they wondered what to do next. Cami decided to join Dee the dumpling kitty and try her luck at the hook-a-duck stall. Pip revealed that she had been asked to star in Suzie the saucepan's Late-Night Acrobatics Show.

'What about you, Lucky?' Pip said.

'I think I'm going to head home and tell my mum all about my special skill!' Lucky said. 'What about you, Sammy?'

Sammy had fallen deeply asleep, thanks to

the oozy, swoozy music of the jelly jazz band.

'Sammy!' they all shouted.

The sloth woke with a start and his fur turned blue. 'On a full moon, a dilly toad can croak louder than a trumpet, you know,' he said.

Lucky laughed. 'You're so tired, you're making no sense at all! Come on, Sammy. Hop up. I'll take you home.'

Everyone gave each other big hugs and promised that they'd see each other again very soon. After more hugs and more goodbyes, Lucky spread her wings, scratched her hoof on the ground and took off into the air.

'See you soon, super cutes!' she called, looking down at Cami, Pip and Dee. They waved

and kept waving until she was out of sight.

Lucky flew up and up into the late evening sky, which was sprinkled with stars and warm with the sun-soaked breezes of Charm Glade. She rode home on blossom scents and the marvellous memories of the Cuteness Competition. What a wonderful day it had been.

Sammy wrapped his arms around her neck and squeezed gently. 'Thank you for today, Lucky. It's been really special,' he said.

'It really has,' Lucky said.

'I was thinking of hosting a little party for my new super cute friends,' Sammy said a little nervously. 'I'm not sure if anyone will want to come. Will you think about it?'

Lucky laughed sweetly. 'I don't have to think at all. The answer is yes, Sammy. Of course we'd love to come. Super cute friends aren't just for a day. They're friends *forever*.'

'Thank you, Lucky,' Sammy said with a sigh. 'That makes me very happy.'

As they rounded a hill, the moon suddenly appeared – full and round, like a gorgeously glowing lantern. Lucky's horn lit up like a beacon, trailing butterfly confetti as she passed through the Marshmallow Canyons towards home.

Far below, baby funny bunnies playing in the grass looked up to see a shimmering confetti shower. They squealed with delight, bouncing and tumbling to catch the

pretty papers as they fell.

'Bedtime,' their mother called.

'But look how cute the world is!' they cried.

Their mother smiled. 'And when you wake

up tomorrow, the world will be cute all over

again. Now, hop it!'

Here's a sneak peek at the next Super Cute book - OUT NOW!

CHAPTER ONE

An Inviting Day!

It was a dazzling day in the World of Cute. The bubblegum flowers had popped at dawn and their strawberry aroma filled the air. Swarms of glass-hoppers dipped in and out of the flower fields and their shiny little wings scattered sun rays far and wide. The spectacle woke everyone from The Marshmallow Canyon to Charm Glade. It even woke Sammy the sloth, who usually snoozed until much later in the day.

Tickled awake by the sparkling light and delicious breeze, Sammy stood at the entrance to Snoozy Hollow, yawned and smiled at the sky.

It's a perfect day for . . . What was it, now? Sammy gave himself a very big wake-up shake . . . It's a perfect day for writing my party invitations!

'Thank goodness for the dazzling morning,' he sighed. 'Or I'd have slept most of the day and missed my dear friend, Louis. He should be here any minute. I must stretch!'

Sammy stepped out and began his sun-salutation yoga routine. He reached high to the candyfloss clouds in the sky, then down to the daisies at his feet, which tried to tickle his toes.

Just as he was getting into a deep stretch, he heard a loud barking. It was nothing to do with his downward-dog position – it was Louis. The labradoodle was running in circles round the meadow.

'Sammy! Sammy! Where are you?' Louis shouted.

Where am I? Sammy pondered. 'Well, in relation to the universe, I'm on a small planet called the World of Cute, but more specifically I am in the area known as the Dipsy Daisy Meadow. If you want to narrow it down further, you could say I was –'

'I can't see you!' Louis called.

Oops! Sammy had forgotten his camouflage

coat was grass-green! He changed his fur to purple, one of his favourite colours. 'Can you see me now?' he asked.

As the labradoodle bounded towards him, Sammy quickly finished his yoga and reached behind to scratch his –

'Fleas, Sammy?' said Louis.

'No, no, no.' Sammy blushed. 'Just an itch on the . . . never mind. How lovely to see you, Louis. It's so kind of you to offer to help with the invitations. Did you bring all your pens and pencils?'

'All right here!' Louis said, tapping his glowing nose.

Sammy had met Louis the labradoodle at

the Blossom Festival, where he had been deftly doodling doodles. And not just deftly doodling doodles, but deftly doodling doodles *with his nose*! Louis had a very special nose, and he was a brilliant artist.

In fact, Sammy had met a *lot* of new friends at the Blossom Festival. That's why he was having a party. And he wanted the invitations to be extra special.

Louis was eager to get started. He pulled a pile of paper from his pocket. 'Shall we begin? What shall I do?'

'First let's decorate the paper,' Sammy suggested. 'Let's make every invitation beautiful, original, different, marvellous, unique . . .'

'You've got it!' Louis said.

The little dog scribbled furiously with his nose. Every time he needed a new colour or a brush instead of a pencil, he simply twitched his nose. Sammy watched with delight.

There were puffs of chalk and sprays of glitter as Louis added the finishing flourishes. Then he stood back, panting as if he'd run a marathon.

Sammy looked down at the beautiful papers laid out on the grass. There were summer scenes, magic whirlwinds, melted colours and dripping rainbows. Each one was a masterpiece. The dipsy daisies began to toss them in the air to dry the ink.

'Wait, dipsies!' said Sammy. 'We haven't done the words yet. Are you ready, Louis?'

Louis twitched his nose into a fountain pen, perfect for writing fancy letters with loops and swirls. Sammy told him what to write.

You Are Invited to
Sammy's Sleepover!
Wear your favourite onesie and bring your favourite toy.
Time: 5pm, this Saturday

'Okay, dipsies, do your thing!' Sammy said, and the daisies tossed the invitations in the air to dry them. They landed back on the grass in a neat pile.

'Bravo!' Sammy cried. 'Let's post them right now.'

'You've forgotten something,' Louis said. 'I haven't written *where the party is*.'

Sammy's eyes shone with mischief. 'Oh!' he said. 'Well, it's a surprise.'

'But we all need to meet *somewhere*,' said Louis.

Sammy chuckled. 'Just put: *Meet at the Wish Tree*. We can walk to the party location from there. No one will ever guess where we're going!'

The extra detail was added to each invitation. Then Louis and Sammy tucked them into golden envelopes and set off to the post box. Louis ran ahead, but returned, his ears flattened with worry.

'The humpygrump hummingbird is nesting in the post box again!' he said. 'I've just seen her pelt Kevin the kettle with poo!'

'Humpygrump poo is the prettiest poo in the World of Cute,' Sammy said. He knew so many facts! 'It has more colours than a rainbow! But also more bad smells than a Stinky Bog Competition. We'll just have to deliver the invitations ourselves. It's a shame I can't walk faster.'

Skye the skateboard trundled to a stop in front of Sammy and Louis.

'Hey, hop on!' she said. 'I'll take you

anywhere you want to go. I've got a bit of free time and four wheels that need exercising!'

As usual in the World of Cute, there was always a perfect solution!

Look out for the next two Super Cute books – COMING SOON!

FUN IN
THE SUN

AND

THE ADVENTURE
SCHOOL

Enjoyed Super Cute? Check out these other brilliant books by Pip Bird!

Books

Join the naughtiest unicorn for friendship and fun!

Look out for more brilliant
adventures with Dave and Mira!

The Naughtiest Unicorn on Holiday

**The Naughtiest Unicorn
in a Winter Wonderland**

COMING SOON!